the SANDWICH THIEF

André Marois　　Patrick Doyon

the SANDWICH THIEF

chronicle books · san francisco

To Lois and Lea, who weren't born yet —A. M.

To A, D + L —P. D.

First published in the United States of America in 2016 by
Chronicle Books LLC.
Originally published in Canada in 2013 under the title
Le voleur de sandwichs by Les Editions de la Pasteque.

Library of Congress Cataloging-in-Publication Data available.

ISBN 978-1-4521-4659-1

Manufactured in China.

English translation by Taylor Norman.
Design by Amelia May Mack.
Font based on handwriting by Patrick Doyon.

10 9 8 7 6 5 4 3 2 1

Chronicle Books LLC
680 Second Street
San Francisco, CA 94107

Chronicle Books—we see things differently. Become part of our
community at www.chroniclekids.com.

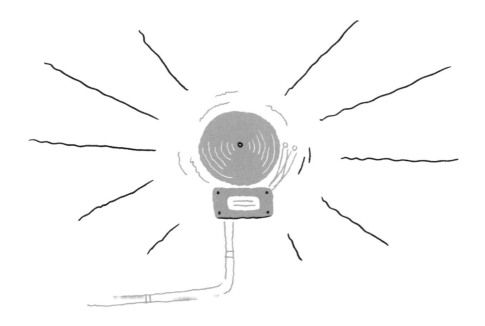

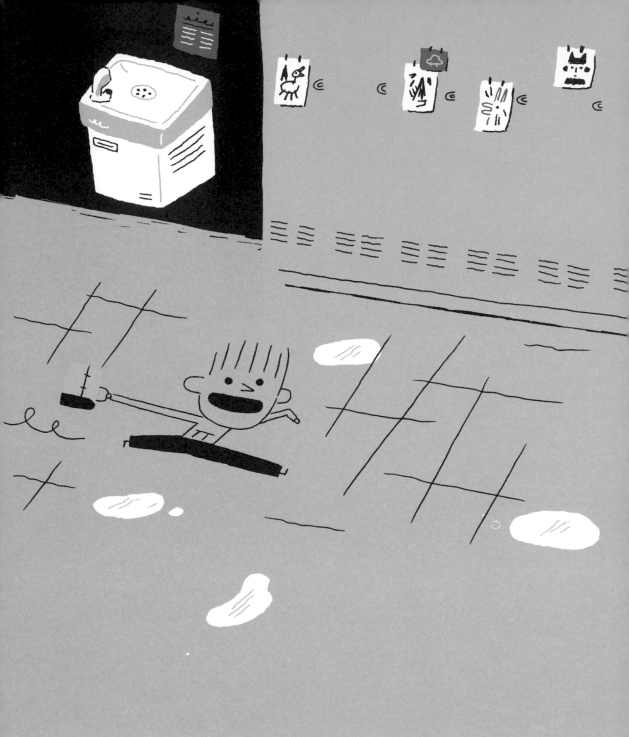

Monday Morning

Lunchtime!

I was the first to stand up when the bell rang.
I rushed out of class, grabbed my lunch box,
and sprinted down the halls to the cafeteria.

We're not supposed to run in the halls, but no
grown-ups saw me. (Still, I was on alert. It had
rained, so I had to look out for the puddles of
water on the second floor.)

As usual, I sat between Axel and Sophie. But:

I dumped my lunch box out on the table.

All that fell out was an apple, a granola bar,
orange juice, and my dad's note. (Papa writes
me a note every day.)

My sandwich is missing.

Are you sure you brought it?

Of course! My Monday sandwich is ham, cheddar, and kale—my favorite.

Someone must have stolen it.

We all looked at each other. Then we looked at everyone around us. It wasn't a pretty sight. Or sound. Everyone was chomping, mouths wide open. You could see little pieces of mashed apple, crushed chips, chocolate chip cookie crumbs. Food everywhere.

I would have recognized my mom's sandwich anywhere. She used fancy bread with special flour that she bought from a secret bakery run by kung fu monks.

I looked across the benches one by one.
For a second I thought I saw my sandwich
between the molars of a big sixth grader,
so I went over to him and pulled down on
his jaw to see if I was right.

HEY, WHAT DO YOU THINK
YOU'RE DOING, NUMBNUTS?

Sandwich
police!

It turned out it
was not my special
Monday sandwich.
Gross. Grocery
store bread.

I collapsed back between my two friends.

So?

My friends, there is a
sandwich thief among us.

"Want a celery stick?" Sophie asked.

I shrugged. I was feeling pretty discouraged.

Monday Afternoon

By that afternoon, my stomach was letting out noisy, embarrassing grumbles. I had never been so starving in my life.

I couldn't concentrate. I watched pieces of paint fall from the ceiling.

One of them fell on Ms. Tzatziki's head.

Everyone laughed.

Except for me.

The theft of my sandwich was totally taking over my brain. What kind of tyrant steals a sandwich? I didn't know what to think anymore. I got mad. Then I got sad. And then I got ready—to track down the culprit.

I decided to make a list of suspects in my notebook.

Number 1: BIG BOBBY

GLUG
GLUG
GLUG

His main hobby is eating.

Sure, maybe at lunch he'd been wolfing down
a huge plate of spaghetti. But I knew Bobby.
Noodles for dessert wouldn't have stopped him
from gobbling up my sandwich as a first course.

Worse still, he ate so much and so quickly that no doubt he'd swallowed it right down without even appreciating it. What a waste.

Grinding my teeth, I watched Big Bobby. I didn't have any proof against him, but he was officially under high surveillance.

Number 2 : POOR MARIE

We all knew her mom had lost her job a while ago. Ever since then, Marie's lunch box had looked more like an empty fridge. So we always shared our lunches with her, which she always accepted, always a little embarrassed.

But Marie would never have stolen my sandwich. At most, she would have taken a tiny bite. Even if she hadn't eaten anything since last week. It was impossible. Right?

I wanted to cross her name off, but I left it. Her lack of lunch made her extremely suspicious.

Number 3: Benjamin
THE ANNOYING

This guy spent his days making up lame pranks that not even lame kids laughed at.

I could picture him unwrapping my sandwich and watching me from a hiding spot, laughing to himself, all alone.

HA HA HA HA HA HA HA HA HA

fake vomit

But I had a feeling Benjamin the Annoying would be interested in a more public joke. He would want everyone to see that he was the funniest. He thought he was hilarious. But he was just annoying.

plastic spider

I put a question mark next to his name.

Number 4: MATHIAS
THE JEALOUS

I knew he hadn't forgiven me for scoring that goal against him in soccer last Friday. Mathias hated when he wasn't the best at something. Our PE teacher was always telling him not to be a sore loser.

So Mathias the Jealous had a great
reason to steal my sandwich: revenge.

I tried to remember. Sevens were the hardest.

I panicked.

Come on, Marin. Ham sandwich
seven times eight?

I could have sworn she'd said "ham sandwich"
this time. Just then, Poor Marie discreetly made
a five and then a six with her fingers.

Why had Marie done that?

I wondered if she was trying to
make up for a certain stolen
sandwich.

Tuesday Morning

My parents are cooking maniacs. They have more cookbooks than clothes and change favorite restaurants more often than napkins. They are foodies, and they're proud of it.

They love a challenge, too. The first week I had my own lunch box, they really outdid themselves. I left each morning with fancy meals with French names. Of course, this immediately made me the fool of the cafeteria.

After that first week, I'd had to sit them down for a talk. "Parents," I said to them. "Please, I beg of you, keep my lunches to a reasonable size with reasonably simple foods." They were disappointed, but they understood my decision. "We want you to be happy every lunchtime," my dad said. But my mom remained firm on one point:

It was a win-win.

When Axel found out my mayonnaise came from my mom's special recipe—eggs beaten with mustard and olive oil—he was amazed. He thought mayo only came from factories.

I was very proud.

Tuesday was the day of my second favorite sandwich: tuna. People never like tuna sandwiches. But this isn't just any old tuna sandwich: It's made with my mom's famous mayonnaise, of course, plus sundried tomatoes.

So I wouldn't die of hunger AGAIN, I decided to lay a trap for the thief. I tied one end of some fishing line to my sandwich bag and the other end to a bell.

If someone went in for the sandwich, they wouldn't see the invisible fishing line, which would ring the bell, and BING!

I ran all the way to school.

I always liked to be the first one there anyway. And today it was especially important.

The hook closest to the door of our class was broken. Darn. My lunch box needed to be as close as possible for me to hear the bell. I hung it on the next closest one.

When class started, I concentrated on the noises in the hall.

9:00 on the dot: A metallic sound—but it was just Benjamin the Annoying trying to juggle two rulers.

9:15: False alarm—Big Bobby dropped his box of candy.

10:17: I leaped out of my seat—

but it was only Mathias the Jealous's music,
which he was listening to secretly.

10:32: Poor Marie jangled her keys in her pocket.

Was everyone in cahoots with the thief?!

Suddenly, the bell dinged against the wall. Ms. Tzatziki looked in the direction of the door and frowned.

I didn't wait for her permission. I rushed out of class.

76

In the hall, there was no one.

The bell was lying on the bench. At the end of the fishing line was my empty lunch box. My marvelous sandwich had vanished.

Nothing was left but the
note from my dad.

The day was off to a bad start.

Going through lunch boxes,
are we?

Fear shot through my body. Mr. Mars stood
behind me with his arms crossed. The janitor
was huge, and his voice always reminded me
of a quiet roaring bear.

I was grumbling all the
way back to my desk.

First conclusion of my investigation: Mathias the Jealous was innocent. Same with Big Bobby, Benjamin the Annoying, and Poor Marie, because none of them had left the room.

But it sure would have been easy for Mr. Mars to take his pick of the most appetizing lunches and help himself.

He could have done the deed, I thought. My empty stomach agreed. Loudly.

Tuesday Afternoon

When the bell rang, I didn't meet Axel and Sophie in the cafeteria. I had a principal to see.

Mr. Geiger was rumpled and unshaven. He looked like he'd slept in his office. It smelled really stuffy in there, too.

Mr. Geiger pointed to the chair in front of him, but I stayed standing.

I wasn't about to tell him this tragedy sitting down. Then I'd be smaller than him.

The principal listened to my story, but he didn't seem nearly shocked enough.

Why didn't you say anything to Ms. Tzatziki?

What can she do? She's a teacher, not the principal.

Mr. Geiger held out a burrito, soft and limp, that he must have bought from the store on the corner. Really unappetizing. If my parents had seen it, they would have accused him of possession and trafficking of junk food and taken him to court.

I tried to push his gross beans back to him.

Um . . . isn't this your lunch?

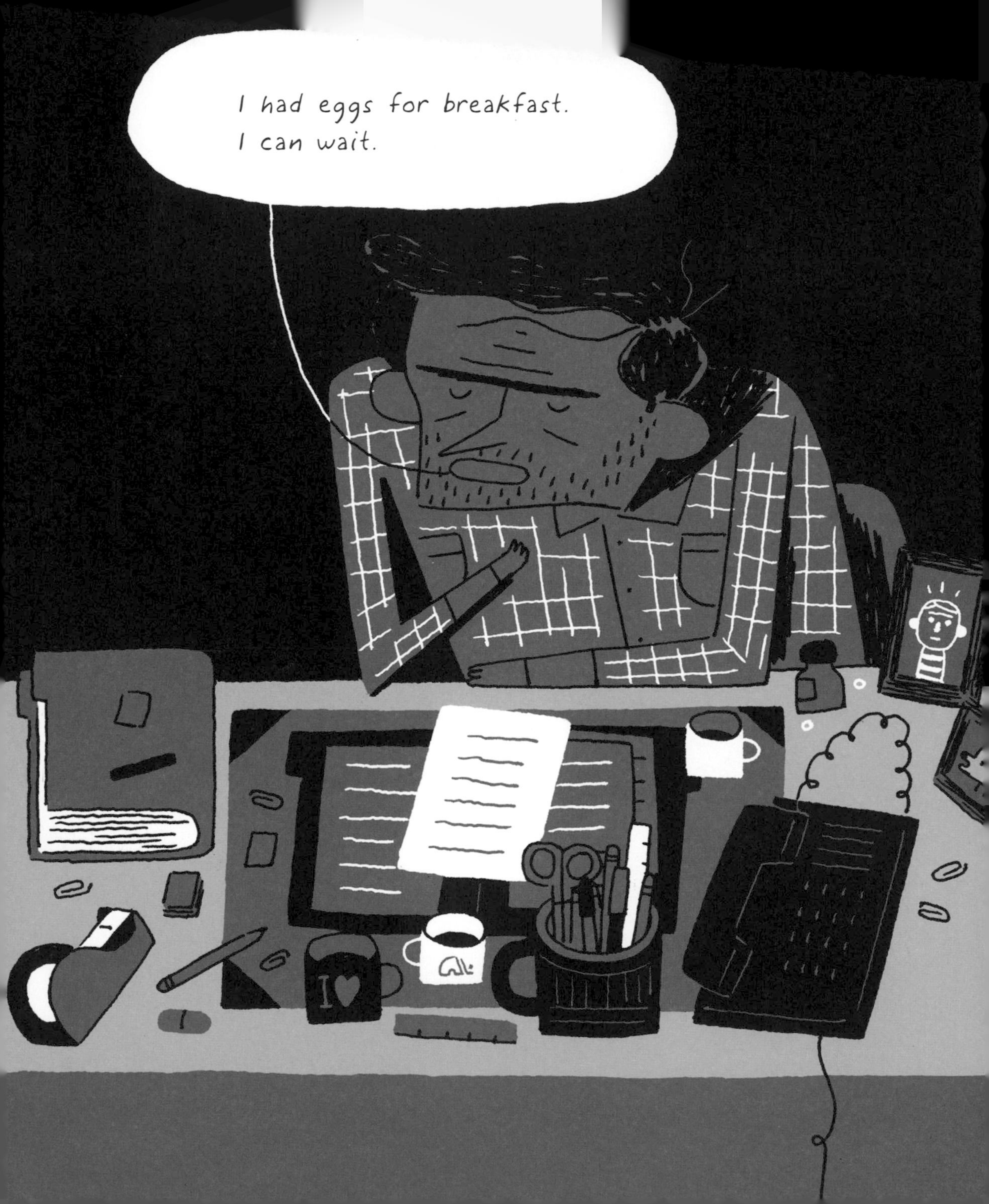
I had eggs for breakfast. I can wait.

Cafeteria food for breakfast?
Store-bought snacks? Apparently,
Mr. Geiger never took time to make
himself a meal. That was a clue. He
definitely had motive to steal someone
else's delicious lunch. Plus, he was the
principal. He made the rules.

Now who was my prime suspect? The
janitor who skulked around the halls or
the principal who didn't care about local
crime and never had his own food?

Wednesday

Every Wednesday, my mom made me an amazing giant shrimp sandwich with alfalfa, tomatoes, and tofu spread.

That morning, I put my lunch box out in the open, to attract the thief.

Mr. Geiger had promised to look into my case, so this would make things simpler for him. Unless he was the guilty one. And even, I realized with a sinking feeling, especially if he was.

The morning passed without much excitement. We were reviewing the past tense of the verb "to have," so I took the opportunity to give an example sentence that would serve as warning to future looters.

Benjamin the Annoying shot
me a black glare.

Mathias the Jealous
pouted.

Poor Marie smiled at
me kind of creepily.

Big Bobby didn't seem
to understand what
was going on.

All crooks, I thought.

At noon, I strolled out of class. No rush. I wasn't going to hurry to collect an empty lunch box.

But my sandwich was still there. I was happy.
And confused. Why today? But I told myself
not to overthink it. My nightmare was over.
Mr. Geiger must have caught the thief. Finally,
I could take Papa's note to heart.

In the cafeteria, I took my place between Axel and Sophie. Sophie was distracted watching Big Bobby, who was sitting across from her, spitting food with every bite. She looked worried. I felt bad for her. I knew what it was like to be afraid at lunchtime. But that made me think of something.

"Hey Sophie, is anyone else in our class allergic to seafood like you?"

"There are four in the whole school. Three students and Mrs. Ohls. I know because our names are on a list in the office."

I almost choked.

I'd known today's lunch was too good to be true. Now I had my true culprit. The teacher of the class across from ours, Mrs. Ohls, must have spied on the hall and snuck out while her students toiled away on some math worksheet. Who would suspect a sweet-looking woman with glasses on a hand-beaded chain?

But the big pink shrimp had kept Mrs. O from gobbling up today's sandwich.

Her allergy had saved my lunch today. But tomorrow?

Thursday

Thursdays were for egg salad sandwiches. They weren't my favorite, because of the smell, but Mom's mayo made any sandwich magic. And the grated Parmesan and red onions didn't hurt either.

I hid my lunch box under Poor Marie's threadbare coat.

No one would expect to find it there. Not even a bandit would stoop to steal from Poor Marie.

Unless that person had absolutely no pity.

Which was entirely possible.

At noon, I was the first out like always. But when I lifted up my lunch box, it was too light. I knew without looking that my sandwich was gone.

I was having a hard time keeping the tears back, I'll admit. Someone in this school wanted to starve me. Or make me crack.

But I wasn't going to let that happen.

I rushed into the teachers' lounge and planted myself in front of Mrs. Ohls. She was *pretending* to correct worksheets.

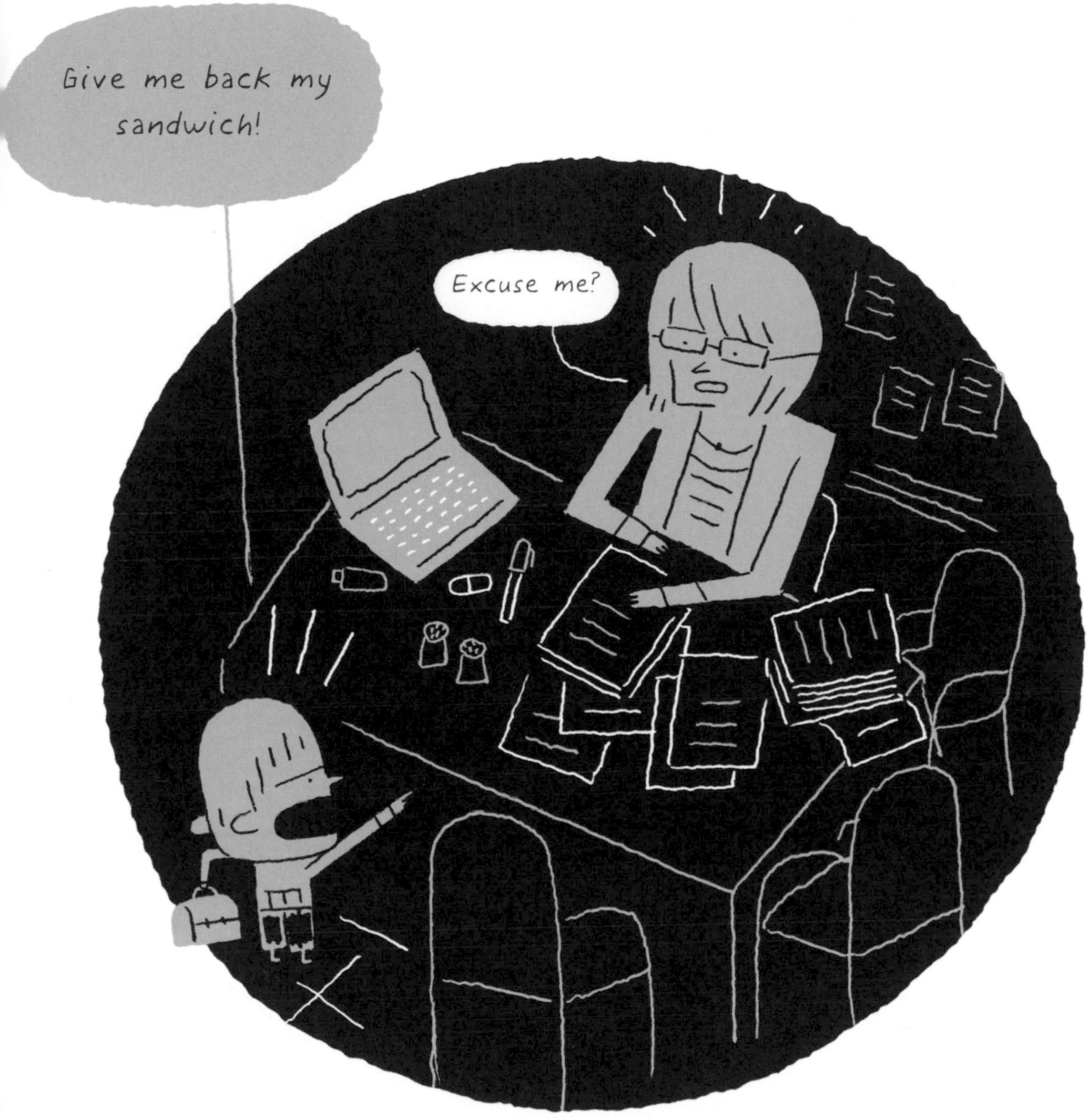
Give me back my sandwich!
Excuse me?

All the teachers looked confused.

I clenched my fists. I was about to scream. But then—

"When you didn't come see me yesterday,
I thought you'd sorted everything out. And
then . . . Well, it's been a crazy morning,"
he said. It was a pretty lame excuse.

But he actually did look busy. I could barely see his desk beneath all the towering piles of paper. There was still some egg on his collar.

That's because yesterday, no one touched my shrimp sandwich. It was there. But Mrs. Ohls is allergic to seafood, so it must be her!

The principal shook his head.

Did he really not know? Or was he
pretending? Was the egg stain on
his collar new?

Egg salad.

A hungry light crossed Mr. Geiger's face.
He was clearly lacking good nutrition. His
skin was a weird color, I noticed.

Mr. Geiger handed me a slice of pepperoni pizza
folded between two pieces of wax paper.

Here, Marin.
At least eat
this.

Man, he was always trying to get rid of gross
food. He was probably just trying to dismiss me
so he could savor the rest of my egg salad
sandwich in peace.

I left with Mr. Geiger's cold, greasy slice, not at all reassured.

In the cafeteria, there was a long line in front of the single microwave, which only worked half the time anyway. I tossed the slice in the trash. It wasn't even worth giving to Poor Marie. I was sure the expiration date on that pizza had passed like eight days ago.

I ate a carrot Sophie handed me and thought. I didn't know who to accuse anymore. And I was so hungry. Today, my dad had written, "I'm thinking of you, my Marin."

We both were.

I tried to imagine what the thief looked like.
All I could come up with was a monster with
Big Bobby's body and three heads: Mr. Geiger,
Mr. Mars, and Mrs. Ohls.

Friday Morning

It was time. I finally told my parents everything.

My mom's eyes lit up. Stealing food from her son was even worse than bringing frozen peach pie to a party. There was going to be trouble!

It's up to us, my Marin. We have to put something in your sandwich that will unmask the thief.

We all thought
about what
ingredient to add.

NAILS!

Papa thought that was a little violent.

Food coloring!

Mom figured the thief would probably notice blue bread.

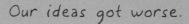

A rat's head.

A fishhook.

Cockroaches.

Toothpaste.

Sand.

Chile pepper.

Wet cement.

A spring.

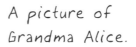
Mold.

A plastic sausage.

A picture of Grandma Alice.

Mom made a special sandwich: chicken, avocado, cucumber, and a thin layer of the famous mayonnaise.

All that was normal.

But then she got out her chemistry kit. Tubes and vials and wires sprung around her face.

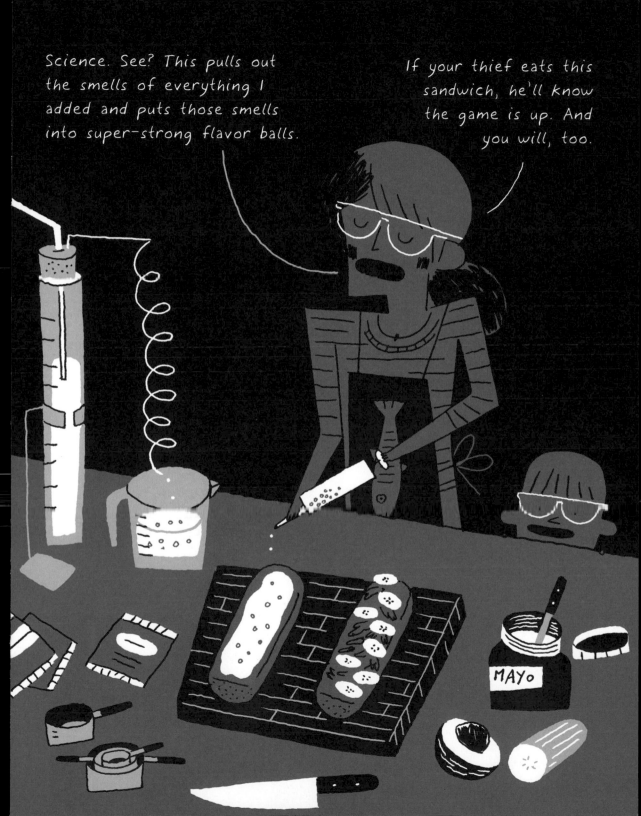

"It's make or break time, my Marin," said today's note.

I put my lunch box on a hook in the middle of all the others and went into class like everything was normal.

Mr. Geiger had promised that today he'd get a grip on everything. If that meant he was planning to get a grip on my sandwich, I'd know soon.

The morning was slow. We started with reading, then did some math. Everything was taking forever. Automatically, I had my eyes glued to the clock above the blackboard, even though it had been weeks since that clock worked.

Suddenly!

I heard a scream in the hall like someone had seen a ghost—then the sound of running feet.

Doors slammed open all down the hall. I sprinted out.

ARRA

My lunch box was lying on the
ground, open, sandwichless.

The scream was still going. Now it was coming from the bathroom.

Inside, Mr. Geiger and Mrs. Ohls crouched over Mr. Mars, who had my sandwich in his hand.

Mr. Geiger pointed at it, worried.

Exactly what did your mother put in that sandwich?

Super-strong flavor balls.

"Flavors of what?" asked Sophie, running up to join us.

Between shivers, Mr. Mars explained.

When I bit into the sandwich, there was an explosion of bizarre flavors in my mouth.

PAH

"The flavors started to fizz, and all of a sudden I could taste dirt, then tar, then soap, then cough syrup, and chalk-textured cat pee, all mixed with vomit."

Mrs. Ohls started to laugh.
Ms. Tzatziki, too.

Mr. Mars kept moaning. Then he rinsed out his mouth again. Then he moaned some more. Then more rinsing.

Looking at the bite missing from my sandwich, I estimated he'd swallowed fifteen flavor balls.

So in one bite, he'd tasted fifteen
dirt-tar-soap-cough-syrup-
cat-pee-chalk-vomit sandwiches.
I almost felt bad for him

It was no wonder he wanted to clean out the disgusting flavor milkshake in his mouth, but unfortunately now the water had stopped coming out of the tap. This happened sometimes because of the old pipes. Like the coat hooks and the microwave, the pipes were another thing Mr. Mars really should have taken care of.

Poor Mr. Mars. He was almost fainting, pointing to his tongue, unable to speak. My mom truly was the queen of food. Or an evil genius.

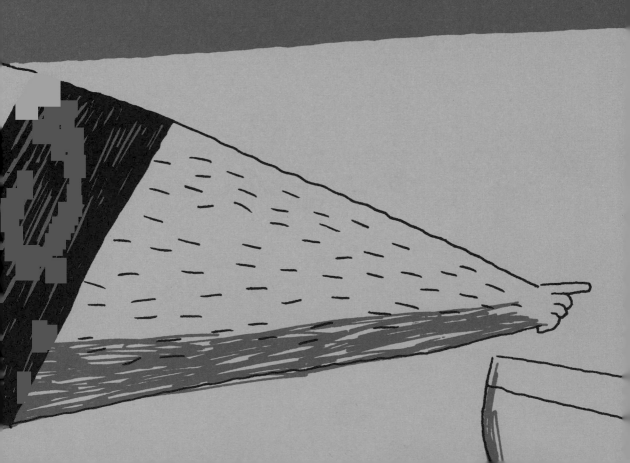

The faucet started to trickle a thin
stream of brownish water. Mr. Mars
kept his mouth wide open below it.

Mr. Geiger handed me the rest of the sandwich.

Why did you do that
to Marin?

I . . . it's nothing against
Marin. But every lunchtime, I would
see him eating those delicious
sandwiches. Just watching him made
my belly grumble and tremble.
It was torture.

But why not . . . be daring,
ask for recipes, and get inspired
to make your own lunches?
I'm sure you could make a . . .
perfectly decent sandwich.

Was Mr. Geiger, world champion of old pizza and
floppy burritos, giving Mr. Mars cooking advice?
Now that was hilarious.

It's the mayo! Marin's mom's homemade mayonnaise. Last week, I tasted just a speck of it that had dripped onto a napkin he'd thrown into the trash, and ever since then, I haven't been able to live without it!

So that was why he didn't steal Wednesday's sandwich! That tofu spread was what had protected my lunch.

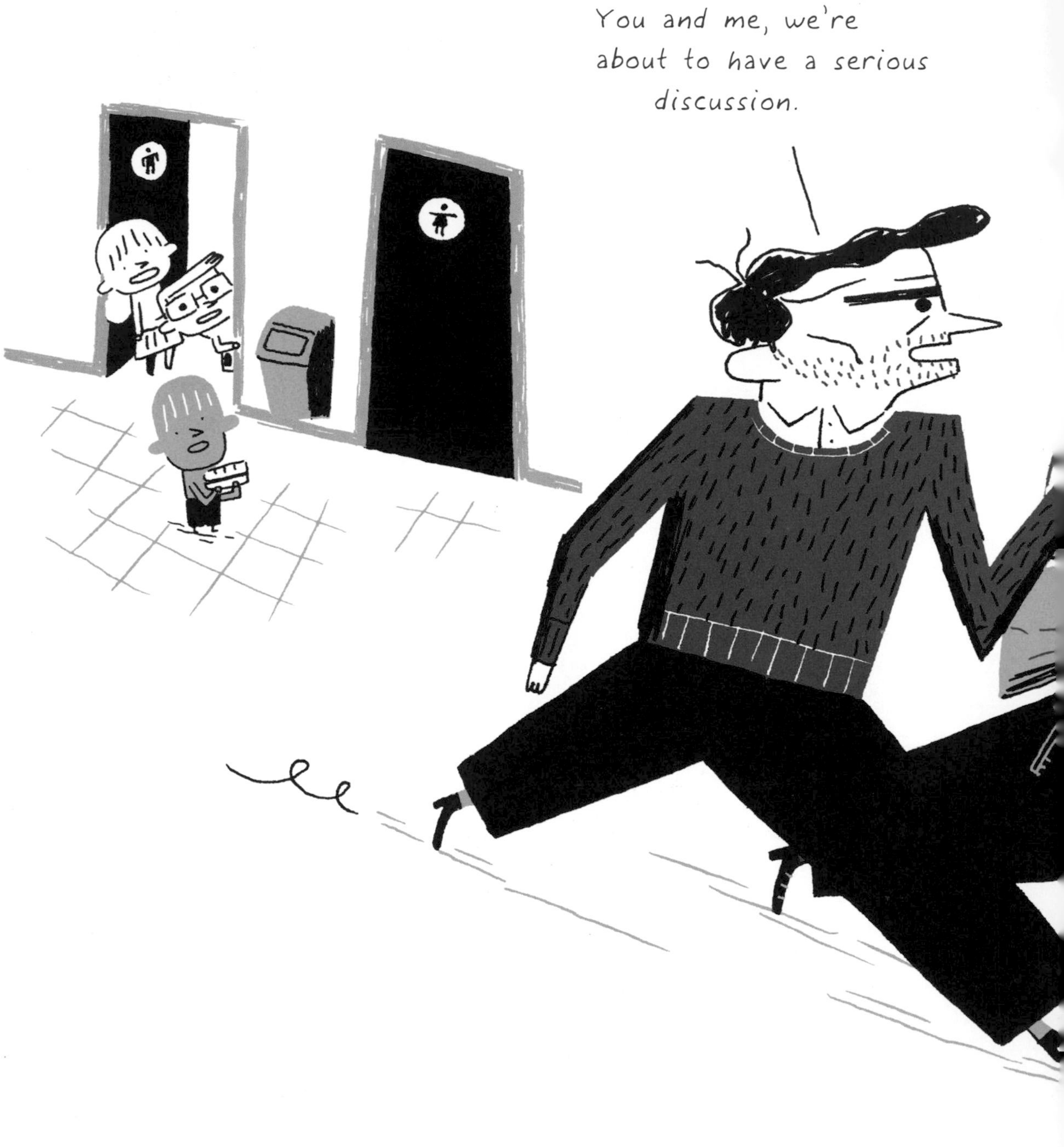
You and me, we're about to have a serious discussion.

I watched them walk off down the hall and tried not to feel too bad. Mr. Mars wasn't getting any less than he deserved. He wasn't my problem anymore.

"What now?" asked Axel.

"Yeah, what now?" asked Sophie.

Well, I for one am starving.
Aren't you guys?

Axel and Sophie looked at my sandwich, chock
full of flavor balls. Then they looked at me like
I was crazy.

No, not *this!* My
mom made me another
sandwich, no tar or dirt
or cough syrup or chalk.
But extra mayo!

Then we ran to the cafeteria before anyone could steal our seats.

Born in 1959 in the suburbs of Paris, France, André Marois is a writer and runs workshops in schools. He's lived in Montréal, Canada, since 1992 and, in addition to being a regular contributor to journals and magazines in Québec and France, he writes crime novels for adults and detective stories for children.

Patrick Doyon is an animator and illustrator with a degree in graphic design from the Université du Québec à Montréal. He was nominated for an Academy Award for the animated short film Dimanche, which was inspired by his experiences growing up in a small town in Canada. In addition to his film work, Doyon is a book and magazine illustrator who has won many awards for his editorial illustrations. The Sandwich Thief is his first book. He lives in Montreal, Canada.